D1541777

Yippy

Written and Illustrated by
ELIZABETH RICE

STECK-VAUGHN COMPANY   •   AUSTIN, TEXAS
An Intext Publisher

To Kay and Harry Sinclair

ISBN 0-8114-7718-5
Library of Congress Catalog Card Number 77-139287
Copyright © 1971 by Steck-Vaughn Company, Austin, Texas

Yippy was a prairie dog.
He lived with his mother
and brothers and sisters in
Prairie Dog Town.

Yippy was a friendly little
animal.

He wanted to see the other
animals who lived in the desert.

He wanted to go to the blue
mountains far away.

Yippy's mother barked
to the pups to come back
to their burrow.
    Yippy hid behind a mound
until all the prairie dogs were
inside their home.

He started out across the desert.

Soon he saw a mound. "A prairie dog mound out here? Prairie dogs always live in towns," said Yippy.

Yippy saw that the mound was
a desert tortoise.

The tortoise moved too slowly.
Yippy passed him without saying
a word.

8

Yippy ran toward the mountains
until he saw two strange birds. He
stopped and stared at them.

9

Yippy met a rock squirrel.
He asked the squirrel about the
strange birds.

"Those are Gambel quail," the
squirrel answered. Then with a
flick of his tail, he disappeared
behind some rocks.

By this time, Yippy was hungry.
He stopped to eat some grass.
    SWOOSH! A roadrunner went by.
A coyote was chasing him.

The roadrunner flew to the top
of a big cactus.

The coyote stopped quickly.

Yippy watched them. He forgot
that coyotes are fond of prairie
dogs for their supper.

Just in time, he saw a hole in
some dried cactus.

Yippy jumped into the hole.
He saw some small sticks, pebbles,
dried leaves, and other things.
He saw an animal smaller than he.

"Who are you?" he asked.

"I'm Packy, the pack rat," the little animal answered.

Yippy asked if he could stay until the coyote went away.

Night came.
Yippy looked out of Packy's den.
He did not see the coyote.

Yippy thanked the pack rat and
started toward the mountains.

He came to a water hole.
He saw animals that he had never
seen before.

Some had horns. Some had long
noses. One animal had a bushy tail.
Yippy was afraid.

He ran away from the water hole.
He heard a strange noise: "Whi! Whi! Whi!"

All Yippy could see were cactus
plants.

23

Then Yippy saw a hole in the cactus.
Looking out were two tiny eyes and a
little head.

"Who are you?" Yippy asked.

"I am an elf owl. I live here,"
said the small bird.

A jackrabbit ran by.

A kangaroo rat jumped past Yippy.

"Run! Run! The gray wolf is coming,"
he called.

Yippy could not run as fast as the jackrabbit.

He could not jump or kick sand like the kangaroo rat.

He would have to hide. But Yippy had no place to hide.

"Quick. Quick. In here, in here," a
voice called.

Yippy saw another bird. It had long legs.

Yippy ran to the hole.
"I did not know that birds lived in the
ground," said Yippy.

"I do," said the bird. "I am a burrowing
owl. This is my home. Once it was a prairie
dog burrow."

Yippy was tired. The mountains were
still too far away.

"You must go home," said the owl.
"I will show you the way. We can
go there in this tunnel."

They went a long way in the tunnel
and came out another hole.

They could see the mounds of Prairie
Dog Town.

"I see my home. Thank you for helping
me," said Yippy.

Yippy ran into his burrow.
"I'll never run away again," he said
to his family.

His mother did not scold him. She
knew that the tired little prairie dog
meant what he said.